Three Lessons for Astair the Bear

by Martin Brennan

illustrations by Amy Huntington

mitten press

All inquiries should be addressed to:
Mitten Press
An imprint of Ann Arbor Media Group LLC
2500 S. State Street
Ann Arbor, MI 48104

Printed and bound in China.

10   9   8   7   6   5   4   3   2   1

Library of Congress Cataloging-in-Publication Data

Brennan, Martin, 1966-
Three lessons for Astair the Bear / by Martin Brennan;
illustrations by Amy Huntington.
p. cm.
Summary: A bear who sometimes has trouble behaving the
way that he should faces three situations from which he learns
to consider the consequences of his actions.
ISBN-13: 978-1-58726-435-1 (hardcover)
ISBN-10: 1-58726-435-8
[1. Behavior--Fiction. 2. Bears--Fiction. 3. Stories in rhyme.]
I. Huntington, Amy, ill. II. Title.
PZ8.3.B74552Thr 2007
[E]--dc22
2006035733

For Mom —M.B.

For Gabe —A.H.

I don't suppose
you've met the bear—
the funny one
they call Astair.
But if you look
inside this book,
you'll find him bumbling 'round in there.

He winds up in
a mess or two
and learns some things
he never knew.
So wander in
and let's begin
these tales I've written just for you.

Lesson One: Bare Facts

One sunny day,
Astair the Bear
woke up
and said,

"**I
do
not
care.**"

He left his house
and didn't care
to wash, or floss,
or comb his hair.

He
walked
along the
thoroughfare
in just his
socks
and
underwear!

He passed a gawking,
gaping mayor

and
five
small
monks in
solemn
prayer.

How the critters
stopped and stared,
but that bold bear
just did not care.
He walked all day,
ran down
some
stairs.

He sauntered
through a
country fair.

Until night fell
and then Astair
smelled something
scrumptious
in the air.

"I'm one tired, famished bear. I need food. I'll go in there."

So walking in, he found a chair. Then waited, and waited, and fumed, and glared.

Until finally
he arose to declare,
"I'm a bear
in need of fare!"

The owner came—
a skunk named Claire,
a skunk with grace
    and savoir faire.

She said,
"You'll
have to go
    elsewhere.

We don't
serve bears
in underwear."

"I'm not leaving,"
growled Astair.
"Your rules—
they're silly
and unfair."

Claire said
calmly,
"Bear beware,"
then raised her tail
high
in
the
air.

"**You wouldn't dare!**"
bellowed Astair.
"**I'm a hungry,**
angry
bear!"

But Claire replied,
"I do not care."

SSSSPPPRRRAAAAYYY

Be very glad
you were not there
to smell the smell
that hit the air…

and see that
choking,
gasping bear,
flailing about
in his underwear.

It took
   six months
      for poor Astair
         to rinse
         that odor
         from
            his
               hair.

But a lesson
    was learned
    by Astair the Bear—
        he never again said,

"I don't care."

Lesson Two: Battered Bones

Astair had made plans for a long, restful trip. He'd set off by train, then he'd sail on a ship.

He'd visit
Vienna,
Versailles,
and Dubai.
But the plans
that we make
at times go awry.

His troubles began
    when he woke up at 9:00.

His train left at 8:00
    and had
        left him
            behind.

"Ah nuts!"

cried Astair.
Then he reached
to the ground
and threw
in frustration
a stone
that he found.

It sailed
through the sky—
how harmless it looked.
Then it fell back to earth

ker-plop in a brook.

The wave that it caused
chased a duck from her nest,
and she QUACKED
as she ran past
an opossum at rest.

QUACK!

QUACK!!

QUACK!!

The
startled old 'possum
jumped up and he fled
past a covey of quail
asleep in their beds.

QUACK!!

And they scared a deer,
and she scared two frogs,
and they scared
nine
mice,
who startled
three
hogs,

and they scared
six chickens,
and they scared
a mare.
And the whole panicked mob
headed straight for…
ASTAIR!

Astair started trembling.
He muttered, "Oh, my."
Then he raised up his paws
and he covered his eyes.

The mob sent
him flying—
how silly he looked—
and he landed head first

ker-plop in the brook.

He bounced off a stone—
the one he had thrown.
Then he lay there
    a moment and
let out a groan.

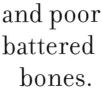

And as for vacation?
He spent it at home,
  nursing his bruises
  and poor
    battered
      bones.

Astair the Bear
loved buying stuff.
He never seemed
to have enough.

His cave was crammed,
could fit no more,
and he was forced

to sleep outdoors.

Which isn't bad
when summer's here.
But wintertime?
He'll freeze his **rear**!

His friends stopped by,
the Squirrel and Moose.
They wondered
had a screw come loose?

Stuff was stuffed,
jammed, squeezed, and stacked,
wedged into nooks,
shoved into cracks—

Collectibles,
old bottle caps,
souvenir mugs,
seashells and maps,
pencils, papers,
five bread bakers,
two juice makers,
twelve salt shakers,
crates of rocks,
and balls of twine,
a portrait of a
porcupine.

Said Moose, "Astair,
why so much stuff?
When will you say
enough's enough?"

"He's right,"
        said Squirrel.
"Bears hibernate.
Clean out this cave.
You shouldn't wait."

"I can't today,"
    replied Astair.
"There are sales—
    big sales—
on underwear."

What happened next,
so I've been told,
the dark night fell.
It grew quite cold.

A fierce wind whipped,
blew ice and snow,

drifts 10 feet deep,
temps 12 below.

Astair trudged home.
He started sneezing.
His teeth ch-ch-chattered.
His toes were freezing.

Now Squirrel
and Moose,
who'd worried so
about their friend
out in the snow,
left their home
to find Astair.

And when they did,
the two just stared!

For there, frozen,
stiff as a stone,
stood poor Astair
outside his
home.

Squirrel gasped. Moose cried,
"The case is dire.
No time to lose!
We'll build a fire."

And so they did.
They built a blaze
from all the stuff
Astair had saved.

The fire roared.
Astair thawed out.
He rubbed his eyes
and looked about.

His cave was clean.
He climbed in bed,
and then he softly,
humbly said,

"My friends, dear friends,
please, no more stuff.
You both were right,
enough's enough!"

And falling asleep,
he dreamt of spring,
of grass, of trees,
of birds that sing.

The winter wind
howled and blew.
Goodnight Astair,
sweet dreams to you.

The End